BATTLE BUGS

THE SNAKE FIGHT

by **JACK PATTON**

illustrated by **BRETT BEAN**

SCHOLASTIC INC.

With special thanks to Adrian Bott

Text copyright © 2016 by Hothouse Fiction.
Cover and interior art by Brett Bean, copyright © 2016 by Scholastic Inc.

All rights reserved. Published by Scholastic Inc., *Publishers since 1920*, 557 Broadway, New York, NY 10012, by arrangement with Hothouse Fiction. Series created by Hothouse Fiction.

The publisher does not have any control over and does not assume any responsibility for author or third-party websites or their content.

ISBN 978-0-545-94512-7

10 9 8 7 6 5 4 3 2 1   16 17 18 19 20

Printed in the U.S.A.   40
First printing 2016
Book design by Phil Falco and Ellen Duda

CONTENTS

SOAPBOX SNAIL

Max Darwin pushed open the door to the garage and grinned. His dad was not an organized person. Unlike Max's bedroom, where the bug tanks were all arranged in neat order, his dad's garage was a mess. Boxes were piled on top of one another. Tools were stuffed into old ice cream tubs.

An abandoned cup of coffee was growing multicolored mold.

Max decided it looked like something out of a disaster movie, where humanity had to survive by salvaging whatever junk it could. Even the corkboard on the wall was covered with random notes, doodles, and designs. But in the entire jumble, one thing in particular stood out. Pinned in the center of the board was a brightly colored flyer. It read:

GRAND SOAPBOX DERBY!
A Day of High-Speed Fun at Hilly Park
Homemade Soapboxes Only—No Store-
Bought Vehicles Allowed!

Max had decided to enter, and soon after, he and his dad had begun working on a design for the soapbox. Now, despite the mess all around them, their hard work had paid off, and they were about to put the finishing touches on their vehicle.

"You need a hand with that?" Max asked, as his dad knocked over a jam jar full of wrenches.

"Oof, sure," his dad grunted. "Let's assemble this thing together."

The soapbox was made from wooden slats taken from an old bed, with four old wheels from a baby stroller. The best part of the whole thing was something Max's dad had found at a yard sale: a huge, hollow, plastic snail shell!

Max thought snails were awesome. Some people confused them for insects, although Max knew that they were actually mollusks. However, that didn't mean they weren't fascinating creatures, and part of the world of mini-beasts he loved so much. Also, it would be kind of funny having what looked like a super-slow snail in a super-high-speed soapbox derby!

Carrying the shell between them, Max and his dad moved it over to the soapbox and carefully lowered it down. Four bolts stuck up from the frame, and with a loud grating noise, the shell slid over them and into place. Max and his dad tightened nuts onto the bolts until the shell was secure.

"It looks amazing!" Max cried.

His dad grinned. "Sit inside and see how it feels."

Max wriggled into the cockpit. The chair had square foam-rubber cushions, which were surprisingly comfortable, and there was an opening in the front of the shell so that Max could steer with a loop of rope.

"It feels great!" he said, steering the front wheels left and right. "But where's the brake going to be?"

"You don't have a brake on an old-fashioned soapbox," his dad said.

"How do I keep from running into a tree?" Max asked nervously.

"You steer around it!" His dad laughed.

I suppose I've got the shell to protect me, Max thought, leaning back. *But still . . .*

His dad knocked on the top of the shell, making a hollow *bonk-bonk* noise. "Come on. Let's load this beauty into the car."

Max hopped out and grabbed one end of the buggy. With his dad grabbing the other side, they maneuvered the whole thing out of the garage. Max tried to focus on what he was doing, but his mind raced and his hands felt sweaty.

This afternoon, he'd be racing downhill. All week he'd been excited, but now that the race was actually here, he felt nervous. The hill was steep, and he'd never attempted something like this before.

He took a deep breath and helped his dad lift the buggy into their SUV. Then he stood on the driveway, going through his mental checklist, while his dad started up the car.

"Oh, wait," Max called. "I forgot one thing."

His dad rolled down the window. "What's the problem?"

"Gimme a minute, Dad. I just need to grab something from my room."

Max bounded inside and ran upstairs. On the desk in his room, he quickly found what he was after. Two long springs with Ping-Pong balls on the ends—the Soapbox Snail's eyestalks! He couldn't go anywhere without those.

As he grabbed them, his hand brushed over his prize possession, *The Complete Encyclopedia of Arthropods.*

Suddenly, he froze on the spot—the encyclopedia's pages were glowing!

He gasped. "The Battle Bugs—they need me!"

The encyclopedia was more than a detailed guide to insects, bugs, and other arthropods of all kinds. It was also a magic gateway to Bug Island, a secret realm where intelligent, talking bugs lived. Max had been there many times, shrinking down to bug size and helping his bug friends in their struggle to survive against the reptile army.

"But I'm supposed to be going to the soapbox derby!" Max groaned. Then he remembered: Time moved differently on Bug Island. Max had often been away for days in the bug world and returned to find that only minutes had passed in the human world.

"Okay, let's do this," he said out loud, as he opened up the encyclopedia. He leafed through the pages until he found the double-page map of Bug Island; light shone up on his face from the glowing pages. There was only one more thing he needed: the magnifying glass that came with the book. He took it out and held it over the map.

Suddenly, a powerful wind whirled around his room, ruffling the curtains and making the paper on his desk fly around in the air. Max felt himself lift off his feet.

"Whoa!" he cried.

The book seemed to grow larger and larger, but Max knew it was actually him that was tumbling down into the pages, through the dark hole that opened up in front of him.

That's strange—the gateway isn't usually dark! Max thought.

But before he had time to worry about it, Max was being whisked through the portal, straight to Bug Island . . .

MISTY MARSHES

Max knew he was heading for something gross. He could tell by the smell: a blend of stagnant water; rotten vegetation; and old, black mud. It was a bit like the smells of a well-used soccer field in the rain. Then, suddenly, came the impact: a *squelch* that left him standing in cold, boggy sludge up to his knees.

"Gross!" he yelled, as he shook dirt off his hands.

Max took a second to get his breath back, then looked around into the nighttime that enveloped him. This was way darker than night ever seemed at home. He took a step forward and then hesitated. With this little light to see by, he could easily blunder into a deep bog or pool and never come out again. Better to take it real slow.

"This is some welcome to Bug Island," he muttered as his eyes slowly adjusted to the dark.

Through the leafy cover overhead, he made out faint stars and a slim crescent of moon. All around lay stretches of black, oily-looking water with patches of firmer ground rising up from it. Reflected stars glimmered in the surface. Farther away into the marsh, a dim blue mist hovered over the water like smoke.

Max decided not to stick around—predators could be anywhere in the dark and he would have no idea. He heaved himself out of the marsh and trudged up to higher, drier ground, leaving a glistening trail of swamp sludge in his wake.

He looked out from the hill, and, suddenly, he knew where he was. "The Misty Marshes!" he said out loud. I've seen these on the encyclopedia map! That means the jungle is . . . this way!"

He peered into the distance, and sure enough, he thought he could make out the silhouette of trees. "If I can just reach the jungle, I can find the bug camp! As long as Barton hasn't moved it again."

The night air was damp and chilly against his skin. Max was dressed for a day at the park, not a night in the marshes. He zipped up his hoodie and kept moving. The outline of the jungle, even blacker than the sky overhead, loomed in the distance.

Max jumped over yet another soggy spot and noticed a strange depression in the ground. There were more little pockmarks and holes nearby. He paused for a while, trying to figure out what kind of bug could have made them, then shrugged and moved on. The Misty Marshes were beginning to give him the creeps.

Suddenly he stopped. A light had flashed up ahead.

Max peered into the distance, suddenly alert.

It flashed again.

"What *is* that?"

Although it was just a tiny flicker against the blanketing darkness, Max's hope grew. Only one thing made a light like that—a firefly! And that meant Max wasn't alone in the dark after all.

Max sprinted toward the light and his grin grew broader as he recognized the glowing insect. It was his trusted friend, the head of the bug underground intelligence network, Glower.

"Hey, Glower!" Max shouted. "I'm glad to see you! I can hardly see a thing out here!"

"No problem!" came Glower's faint voice shouting back to him. "I'll come to you! Don't go near the . . ." His voice faded away.

"Near the what?" Max hollered, but Glower's words were lost on the night air. Max gritted his teeth and ran on toward Glower's light.

The firefly zoomed toward him. Glower was flying so low he was almost brushing the ground. Suddenly, though, something burst out of the ground from one of the dark holes. It was snakelike, reptilian, and moved with a hunched wriggle that made Max feel sick with fear.

"Glower, watch out!" Max shouted.

"Huh?" Glower said.

The reptile twisted around to glare hatefully at Max. He had never seen anything like it before. It had a long, scaly body and a stubby little head, just like a snake. But it also had small, clawed forelimbs, just like a true lizard.

A Mexican worm lizard!

The worm lizard lunged up at Glower, chomping and scrabbling. The firefly darted out of the way, but not quickly enough.

"Another tasty morsel," the worm lizard hissed in delight.

"Max, get out of here!" Glower shouted, as the reptile grabbed him by the leg. A

quick tussle, a sudden tug—and Glower's light vanished.

"No!" Max yelled. He ran to the hole.

The light from Glower was plummeting down, getting smaller and smaller as the worm lizard dragged him away. Max caught a glimpse of Glower's panicked face. Then he was gone.

Max stood for a second, numb with shock. Then he pulled himself together. Glower needed him. He had to find the others, *fast*.

He ran to the edge of the jungle and headed between the massive trees, looking for the bug camp. To his relief, it wasn't long before he caught sight of the termite towers looming above the forest floor. The bug sentries saw him first, and Spike the emperor scorpion came dashing out to give him a ride the rest of the way.

"Max, you're back!" Spike said happily. But soon, he saw the stern look on Max's face, and knew something was wrong. "What is it? What happened?"

"We need Barton, now!" Max said, hurrying into the Battle Bugs' camp.

Soon after, Max stood before the Battle Bug command team: Spike, Webster the trap-door spider, Buzz the hornet air ace, and, of course, General Barton, the titan beetle who led the bug forces. Nearby sat Spotter, the dragonfly who'd helped Max beat back the crocodile forces on his last visit.

Still breathless, Max told the bugs about the worm lizard snatching Glower.

"I feared the worst when Glower failed to report for duty," Barton said, gravely.

"Have things been bad here?" Max asked.

"Well, the river patrols you suggested have been working out great," said Spotter. "No sign of any crocs—"

"Yes," Buzz interrupted. "But Glower isn't the first bug to go missing . . ."

Barton nodded. "We've heard reports of bugs being hauled underground and never seen again. But until now, nobody had seen the culprit up close."

"The worm lizard," Max said. "It must have snatched all those other bugs, too!"

"Exactly," rumbled Barton. "Now that you're here, Max, and we finally know what we're up against, it's time to take action."

"Let's form a search party to look for the missing bugs," Max said instantly.

Spike snapped his pincers in the air. "Yes! I knew Max would get right to work. Didn't I tell you, Buzz?"

Max paced up and down, thinking about whom to have on the team. "Webster, can you come? We could use your web lines to help us climb down the hole."

"If you're sure I w-won't get in the way," said Webster, nervously.

"I'll come too, sir!" squeaked a voice from the back of the cave.

Max looked over and saw a very strange sight—a set of glowing feelers waving over the other bugs' heads.

"Ah, Cadet Roxy," boomed Barton. "Move aside, bugs. Let her through."

Max watched openmouthed as Roxy slid toward him on multiple legs, casting light all around her. She was a millipede, and her entire body was glowing with a pale, soft light.

"I can climb and I light up," she explained, "and I have some other tricks, too."

Max thought for a second. Roxy's luminescence would be perfect for the mission.

"Welcome aboard!" Max said.

The millipede beamed even brighter in delight.

Max organized the bugs, and, soon, he, Webster, and Roxy set out from the bug camp on the rescue mission. Spike stayed behind to patrol the perimeter with Barton and the other forces.

Max marched in front, ready for action.

"Remember the Battle Bugs' motto," Max said. "Never leave a bug behind! So, let's go find Glower!"

RESCUE MISSION

Max, Roxy, and Webster cautiously made their way out of the jungle and across to the edge of the swamp. Max knew Glower was counting on him—the Battle Bugs were the only ones who could save him now.

He kept glancing across at Roxy. With her glowing, semitransparent body gliding up and down the humps of earth, she made for a strange sight. Shadows shrank and lengthened as she passed by.

"How do you do that?" he asked her. "I know fireflies like Glower can light up their abdomens, but that's just one part of their bodies. You're glowing from one end to the other!"

"It's called bioluminescence," Roxy said proudly. "The chemicals in our bodies react to produce light. All the millipedes in my genus have it."

"What genus is that?"

"*Motyxia*!" said Roxy. "And that's not all. We're poisonous, too—all over!"

"Wow!" Max said. "So I shouldn't touch you, right?"

"Right!" Roxy said. "Unless you want to be seriously knocked out—"

Roxy was so caught up in her conversation with Max that she nearly blundered into the big, dark hole in front of her. Only Webster's quick reaction saved her from falling over the edge.

"Oops!" Roxy gasped, steadying herself and waving her feelers around. "I get a little carried away sometimes."

"C-careful!" Webster whispered. "W-we don't want to lose another bug!"

The three of them gathered around the edge of the hole. It looked crumbly and dangerous. Not one sliver of light penetrated its depths.

"Is this w-where the worm lizard took Glower?" Webster asked.

"I'm certain of it," Max said. "See those claw marks in the ground? The worm lizard made those. Glower's down there somewhere, and hopefully so are the other missing bugs."

Webster peered down the hole. "It looks dark and deep, Max. Normally, I like it underground, but only in holes I've dug myself!"

"In that case, Roxy's definitely the right bug for the trip," Max said. "We're going to need all the light we can get."

Max explained his plan to the others. "We're going to lower ourselves down the hole, one by one. Webster, we'll need plenty of silk."

"No problem," he whispered.

"I'll go first!" Roxy volunteered. "I can light up the way."

"Good thinking," Max said. "Webster, spin a silk loop around Roxy and lower her down. We need to do this fast. There might be more worm lizards around."

Webster quickly went to work with his spinnerets. In less than a minute, Roxy went scrambling over the edge of the pit—this time on purpose. She hung in space, dangling by a single webbing thread that gleamed in the light from her body.

"Good to go!" she said, and gave Max a little salute.

Webster let out more and more silk, gradually lowering Roxy down the hole.

Max watched her slowly descend into the darkness. Strange noises from nearby made him jump: a scraping noise that might be a reptilian claw, a quiet hiss that might be a predator waiting to attack. The Misty Marshes had lost none of the creepiness from his last visit.

"Can you go any faster?" he asked.

"I'm going as fast as I can," Webster panted.

Max was sure it wasn't fast enough. He was beginning to think something was watching them.

Eventually, after what felt like hours, the faint call finally came: "I've reached the bottom!"

Max peered down and saw Roxy waving from far below, looking tiny as a glowworm.

"Great! Now my turn," he told Webster.

Webster spun out some silk. Max took the gluey, sticky stuff in his hands and held it to his waist. Then, he spun around until it was securely wound around him like a belt. He wouldn't fall out of *that* in a hurry.

Webster braced himself to take Max's weight. Max climbed over the edge of the pit. Fragments of earth broke away in his hands and he fell, tumbling silently, into the dark.

Max gulped. He steadied himself with his legs against the shaft wall and began the slow descent.

It wasn't as easy as he'd expected. Webster's line came in fits and starts, which made Max bounce about jerkily, like a toy on a string. He tried to use his legs to control his descent, but he couldn't see what he was doing in the dark. He'd bounce off the wall, spin around in the middle, and then bounce off the opposite wall.

"Hang in there, Max!" Roxy called. "You're doing fine!"

"Thanks," said Max feebly. All the spinning was making him feel dizzy.

"Not far to go now," he said to himself. "If I can just . . ."

"Max!"

Suddenly Webster's terrified voice came from above. "Something's up here with me!"

"Uh-oh," Max said. "Pull me up as quick as you can!"

Webster began to wind in his silk, but it was no use. Max kept spinning and bouncing off the walls. Webster was panicking.

"They're coming, Max. I can see them," Webster cried. "T-two of them. Worm lizards!"

Max looked down. Roxy was turning in anxious circles, watching him hang in midair. He knew that he'd never make it in time. Webster would have to make a run for it, and that meant he'd have to cut the silk rope.

Max was bug size now. That meant he could survive drops that a full-size Max never could—he hoped.

"Webster, cut the line and run!" he shouted.

"N-no!" Webster shouted. "You'll fall!"

"You have to do it; there's no other way," Max cried.

Webster wouldn't do it—there was no way he'd let Max drop. So Max would just have to do it himself.

He rummaged around in his pocket until he found what he was after: a screwdriver! Finally, all the chaos of his dad's garage had come in handy.

He set to work breaking the sticky web, jabbing and twisting as quickly as he could. This was just like when he'd been stuck in Jet the black widow spider's webbing, so he knew the best way to get through the spider silk. Eventually, only a tiny sliver of silk remained.

"Here goes nothing," Max cried, slicing the rope. Suddenly, Max was hurtling through the air with a *whoosh* toward Roxy's faint light.

Smack!

The impact knocked the wind out of him. His legs buckled. Roxy crowded round him, her feelers quivering nervously.

"Ouch," Max gasped. "That one hurt."

He clambered to his feet and looked up toward Webster. He couldn't see a thing. "Webster, are you okay?"

"I'm sure he made it," Roxy said. "I saw him scurry away."

"I hope so." Max sighed. "Can you bring your light over here?"

Roxy shuffled forward, casting her bright glow over him, and stopped. "Whoa. What is that? You're covered in slimy goop. That's not human blood, I hope."

"What? No! Our blood's red." Max held up his hand and saw that it was coated with some kind of transparent slime. A slow, gluey drop fell from it as he stared. He glanced down and saw that his knees were coated, too. *I must have landed in it,* he thought.

Roxy moved in figure eights, lifting her legs up. Sticky, silvery trails stretched between them and the floor. "Ugh. What is that stuff? It's all over the cavern."

Before Max had a chance to wonder what it was, Roxy let out a terrified squeal.

Max turned to look at what Roxy had spotted. He looked up . . . and up . . . and up at the shadowy *thing* that was towering over him.

Something was emerging from the darkness, a presence more vast and strange than anything he'd ever seen before on Bug Island . . .

SLIMY SECRETS

"We need to get out of here," Max called.

"I think you're right!" Roxy cried.

They tried to run away from the massive shadow gliding slowly toward them, but they didn't get far. The slimy sludge underfoot was thick as molasses, and Max's sneakers skidded and slipped. With a yell, he fell headlong into the stuff.

"Max, come on!" Roxy urged, twisting around to look back at him.

Max found himself floundering on his back. Using his hands and feet, he shoved himself backward through the slime. He had to get away from the oncoming presence.

Roxy ran back across to him to help. By the light of her body, Max finally got his first good look at the creature towering over him.

It was a gigantic snail! Its head was a thick, glistening mass that slowly swayed from side to side, and its shell was a twisting cone, set with spikes, rising high into the cavern. The sheer size of it took Max's breath away.

"I know what that is," he said in a whisper. "But it can't be—it's not possible!"

The gigantic snail oozed steadily forward, its grayish-white body looming like an oncoming ocean liner.

"It's the largest snail that ever existed," Max stammered to Roxy. *"Campanile giganteum."*

The snail's giant head craned down to peer at Max. A great rubbery slit of a mouth gaped at him, full of strange comblike rows of teeth. And then it smiled.

"What a polite little thing you are," it said, in a deep booming voice that echoed through the caverns.

"Excuse me?" Max asked.

"You know my full name! I must say, it's been a very long time since anyone addressed me by that title. A very long time, indeed." The snail bowed its head. "Most people call me Slimer."

"Slimer," Max echoed. "It's nice to meet you. I'm Max."

"And I'm Roxy," Roxy said.

"Hmm," Slimer said thoughtfully. He looked Max up and down. "In all the forty million years that my family has lived, I have never seen nor heard of a creature like you before. What are you?"

"I'm a human," Max explained.

"I see. Do you find me strange, Max the Human? Your eyes are very wide."

"I don't mean to be rude," Max said, careful not to offend the ancient snail. "It's just that where I come from, we haven't seen anything like you, either. Not for millions of years."

"I haven't, either!" Roxy jumped in.

Slimer nodded his head in a knowing way. "Bug Island is a magical place. The caves and tunnels run deep here. Many of us Old Ones live down here now, peaceful and undisturbed, content to dream through the long centuries, far away from our original homes." He sighed. "At least, that was how it used to be. Things are changing now."

Before Max could ask Slimer what he meant, Roxy asked a question of her own.

"There have been lots of bug disappearances around here. I was wondering if you'd seen any strange bugs? Or maybe any reptiles . . . worm lizards, perhaps?"

"Hmm," Slimer said in an absent-minded kind of a way. "Strange things have been happening. Flooding in some tunnels, cave-ins in others. The very lowest caverns are not safe anymore." His head drooped and his mouth sagged. "Many of us have been pushed closer to the surface. It is hardly fair, isn't it? We only want to be left alone."

Max and Roxy glanced at each other. Something about Slimer's words was making Max uneasy. There were many natural events that could cause caverns to collapse. But there were so many holes dotting the surface, Max feared there was something else going on, something not natural at all.

"My friend Glower was dragged down here earlier," Max told Slimer. "We need to find him and the other missing bugs, but we don't know where to start. Can you help?"

"Help?" Slimer boomed. "Of course I can help! Why, I know the tunnels down here like the back of my own shell."

"Awesome," Roxy said. "Never leave a bug behind!"

Max let out a sigh of relief. Finally, it seemed like the bugs' luck was changing.

"We'll find your friends in no time," Slimer said, oozing toward one of the tunnel openings. "Follow me!"

Max and Roxy followed eagerly as Slimer slithered down a narrow tunnel. His enormous body almost touched the sides, but the pair of them just managed to squeeze alongside him.

Soon after, they came to a stop. After only a few hundred feet, the tunnel had come to a dead end. The three of them looked at the solid earth wall in front of them.

"Hmmm!" Slimer said. "I could have sworn . . ."

"Are we lost?" Max asked.

"No, no, no," Slimer said. "Let's just go back and try again."

They backtracked and followed Slimer through the next tunnel entrance. Soon, they were following the tunnel down in what felt like a gentle spiral.

"Oh, no," Slimer said again as they came to another sudden stop.

"What is it this time?" asked Max.

"See for yourself," Roxy muttered.

Max pushed past Slimer's flabby flank and looked out across the cavern they'd entered. A huge ravine, plunging down too deep for him to see the bottom, stretched in front of them. It completely blocked their path.

"What on earth is that doing there?" Slimer exclaimed. "The Crystal Cavern is supposed to be back the other way."

"Back to the start and try again?" asked Roxy.

"Come on, dawdlers!" Slimer announced. He slowly turned around on the spot and slid back the way they'd come. "We'll find the, ah . . . what were we looking for, again?"

"The captured bugs," Max said in desperation. He was beginning to think Slimer had no idea where they were going.

"Yes. Of course: the captured bugs. We'll all be nibbling leaves together by tomorrow at lunchtime; just see if we don't!"

Two more dead ends later, Max and Roxy were boiling over with frustration. It was bad enough that Slimer moved about as fast as a bicycle with square wheels, but his absent-mindedness made it even worse.

"I thought he said he knew these tunnels

like the back of his own shell!" Roxy whispered.

"You know," Max began, "I don't think he's ever *seen* the back of his own shell."

Roxy laughed.

Eventually, after they'd wandered around in the semidarkness some more, they came to a fork in the tunnel.

"We go left here," Slimer announced. "I distinctly remember seeing strange-looking creatures pass this way."

He sounded totally confident, but then again, he'd been confident about the "shallow little pool" that Roxy had nearly drowned in, and the "perfectly secure bridge" that had collapsed under Max's weight.

"Looks abandoned to me," Roxy said. "What do you think, Max?"

Max looked left and right. To the right was a cozy-looking tunnel whose roof and walls were securely held together with tangled tree roots. To the left was a flinty, steep passageway decked with ancient cobwebs.

"If Slimer says go left, we go left," Max said wearily. "He's got to be right sooner or later."

"I hope so," Roxy said.

They followed Slimer down an ever-widening passageway that became a massive cavern. The echo of dripping water resounded from far off in the dark. There were no exits anywhere that they could see. Max glanced up and saw the pointed, spear-like tips of large stalactites hanging from the ceiling.

"There's no sign of Glower here," he said. "This place is giving me the creeps."

"Agreed," Roxy said firmly. "Come on, Slimer. We're going back."

The giant snail began his slow, slow turn. Max ground his teeth in frustration. But then, in an instant, a strange vibration went from the ground, through his feet, and all the way up to his head. The air felt hot and the tunnel seemed to be shaking on all sides.

"Uh-oh." Slimer groaned.

"What is that?" Roxy yelped.

Another vibration came, this one much stronger than the last. The next moment, Max was thrown off his feet, and the ground began to shake violently.

"Earthquake!" he cried.

CAVE-IN!

"Grab on to something!" Max yelled.

The shaking got worse and worse. A loose rock smacked painfully into the back of Max's head and bounced off across the cavern floor. More and more rocks followed, striking his back and shoulders as if it was raining pebbles.

"It's a cave-in," Roxy cried. She darted

back and forth, desperately looking for shelter. Lumps of rock and earth slammed down around her.

The tremors grew stronger. It sounded like two stone jaws grinding together. Max and Roxy were flung around like beetles in a shaken matchbox.

Max remembered the stalactites and looked up, just in time to see a length of stone crack free. It fell toward him, fast as a javelin. He rolled out of the way just in time. The stalactite crashed down, inches away from him, and shattered into chunks.

He sprang to his feet. "That was close," he panted.

"Take cover, everyone!" boomed Slimer, as the rain of rocks became even heavier.

"Where?" Max yelled. "There's no way out!"

"Over here!" Slimer called. Quick as a flash he drew his head back into his cone-shaped shell, retreating farther and farther. He squeezed back so far inside that there was enough room for Max and Roxy to climb in there with him.

Max huddled up against Slimer's clammy body as bits of stalactite pinged off the snail's armored back.

Roxy trembled. "Are you sure we're safe in here?"

"Perfectly safe," Slimer assured her.

Max flinched as a heavy rock spike shattered against Slimer's shell. He told himself he was safe. After all, Slimer had lived down in these tunnels for many years. Surviving was something he was good at.

Eventually, the falling stones slowed to a trickle and the ground stopped shaking.

"I think it's stopped," Roxy whispered.

Slimer pushed down with his body, lifting his shell enough for Max and Roxy to scramble out.

The cavern was transformed. Instead of the humped rock floor with occasional stalagmites, there was a mess of fallen rock, sand, and loose earth. Many of the stalactites had broken off and fallen, and now lay in sharp shards across the ground. It looked as if a crane had swung a wrecking ball through the place.

Slimer, they now saw, was half-buried in debris. He slowly emerged from his shell as if he were waking up from a long nap. "See, I told you we'd be fine."

We were nearly killed, Max thought.

"Look!" yelled Roxy excitedly. "Over here!"

Max ran over to her, his feet crunching on the freshly fallen gravel. Roxy had found an exit—a narrow one, but an exit nonetheless. Somehow, the earth tremor had helped them find the way, when all of Slimer's years of knowledge had failed. Max looked down at the loose rocks littering the ground nearby.

"I guess this tunnel must have been

blocked off, and the tremor shook the rocks free," he said.

"That explains why we didn't see it before," Roxy agreed.

"Aha! That's definitely the right way," said Slimer as he glided over. "That's where those worm lizards took your bugs! I knew that opening was here somewhere."

"We never doubted you for a second," Max said smoothly.

Roxy just laughed.

Max climbed into the tunnel. The ceiling was low, so he had to crouch down. Roxy slid into it on her many legs with no trouble at all.

"Scoot over, you two!" called Slimer. He crammed himself against the hole. Most of his head squeezed into it, but the rest of him was just too big.

"I don't think you're going to fit," Max told him.

Slimer's eyestalks wobbled as he strained at the opening. "You can't give up that easily! Young people these days have no backbone, that's the trouble."

"I'm the only one here who *does* have a backbone," Max muttered. "One of you is a mollusk and the other one's an arthropod!"

Slimer pulled his head out. "I'm going to try going in shell-first," he said. "We'll get there in the end, don't worry."

Roxy hid her eyes. "I can't watch. Tell me when it's over."

Max backed away down the tunnel. The

pointy tip of Slimer's huge shell appeared. It slowly advanced on them, filling more and more of the tunnel, until—with a dramatic *crunch*—it got stuck.

"Hello?" came Slimer's muffled voice. "Are you still there?"

"Yes!" Max shouted.

"I think we need a change of plan," Slimer said.

"Right," Max said.

"I'll stay here and guard the cavern," Slimer called, "and you two go on without me."

"Sounds like a good idea," said Max. He grinned at Roxy.

"Good luck. I'll guard this place with my life!"

Max and Roxy hurried down the passageway. Max felt sad to be leaving Slimer, but he knew that having him guard the entrance to the tunnel would keep him and Roxy safe.

The tunnel snaked through rock and earth, under fronds of hanging roots and around bulging masses of flint, until it came to a short, steep upward slope. Max was about to climb it when he heard a low, hissing voice uttering faint words.

Reptiles! he thought, suddenly alert. He held up his hand, signaling for Roxy to stop, and pulled himself a little way up the slope so he could peek over the edge.

Down on the other side was a bowl-like cavern, with pools of water dotting the floor. Greenish-white spots of fungus that gave off a dim and eerie light had formed on the walls. *More bioluminescence*, Max thought. It happened in the fungus kingdom as well as the animal.

The light was faint, but it was enough for Max to see the creatures that had spoken. He held his breath. Three snakelike beasts with tiny, clawed forelegs were huddled together next to one of the pools, drinking from it in little sips and talking to one another.

"Worm lizards," he whispered over his shoulder to Roxy. He recognized one of them as having snatched Glower. "Three of them."

"Can you hear what they're saying?" she asked.

"Not from here. We need to get closer."

"But they'll see us coming!"

Max saw what Roxy meant. The light from her body would be visible all the way across the cavern. Nobody would mistake the millipede for a glowing fungus.

He pulled his hoodie off—it was still damp from Slimer's slime—and draped it over Roxy. He tucked the hood down over her head and tried not to laugh at how strange she looked.

"That ought to do it," he said. "Don't move too quickly or it'll fall off."

"You humans are weird," Roxy muttered. "It took me *ages* to shed my skin when I was small. You just pulled yours off in seconds!"

Max just laughed. "It's not quite the same thing . . ."

He and Roxy climbed up the slope and carefully picked their way down the other side. The worm lizards were still next to the shallow pool.

Slowly Max and Roxy crept forward, hiding behind boulders and bulges in the cave wall, until they were close enough to hear what the worm lizards were saying.

"The new bug is bold," said one. "He keeps insulting me. I'll have to give him a lesson in manners, I think."

Glower, thought Max.

"No!" hissed another lizard. "No matter

how annoying—or delicious—the bug captives are, we must not eat them!"

"But I'm hungry," groaned the third lizard. "There's so little to eat in these tunnels."

"The bugs are for our master, remember?" hissed the second lizard. "Think how pleased she'll be when she sees them. That's what we've been working for. Think what a mighty ally she will be for the reptile army."

The worm lizards chuckled to themselves.

Don't stop now, Max thought desperately. *Keep talking . . .*

"Will this offering be enough?" asked the first lizard.

"It will be enough to remind her how sweet bug-flesh is," said the second. "When her appetite is awakened, she will be sure to come to the surface with us, to help us conquer the bugs once and for all."

"The bugs will surrender in terror, once they see who is coming for them!" gloated the third lizard. "They cannot have forgotten the name of Lieutenant Titan!"

The moment she heard that name, Roxy let out a squeal of pure fear.

And in that instant, three pairs of tiny black eyes glared at them, full of hatred . . . and hunger.

CAPTURED

"Run!" Max yelled.

With Roxy close behind, Max ran for his life. The worm lizards gave chase, slithering across the rocks more quickly than he could have imagined. They reached for him with their hooked claws.

He reached the upward slope and took it

at a run. From behind came a startled squeal as one of the worm lizards caught Roxy.

"Keep going!" she screamed to Max.

Max turned—he wasn't about to leave a bug behind. He pulled out his screwdriver and faced the other two lizards. All too quickly they were on him, grabbing with their sharp claws and dragging him backward. He slashed at them with his weapon, but soon they had him held fast in their grip. Their scaly, wormlike bodies pressed up against his—there was no escape.

A worm lizard's ugly face loomed in front of his own. "You're no bug. Are you on their side?"

"He's not with me," Roxy bravely tried to say, but the worm lizard holding her covered her mouth with a claw.

"I'm Max," he said defiantly.

The worm lizard started at the sound of his name. "I've heard of this one: Barton's special adviser. We're in luck. Our special banquet for Lieutenant Titan just got a whole new course!"

Max struggled in the creature's clammy grip, but it was no use. All he could do was let himself be dragged along to his fate.

The worm lizards took Max and Roxy all the way to the back of the cavern and down a short tunnel. Up ahead, Max saw something that made him stare.

There was a wide hole in the floor, covered with a layer of what looked like reptile skin. It must have come from something at least the size of General Komodo, judging by the size of it. Rocks had been dragged into position around it, holding it secure like a tarpaulin. A dim, greenish light shone through the skin from the other side.

One of the worm lizards, grumbling, moved rocks out of the way until he could lift a corner of the skin and make an opening. "Chuck 'em in with the others," he growled.

The two other worm lizards bundled Max and Roxy down into the pit below. Once they were through, the reptiles weighed the skin down with rocks again. Max shoved it as hard as he could, but it was tight as a drum skin.

"Don't bother trying," laughed a worm lizard. "That skin's tough as Lieutenant Titan herself. It ought to be—she shed it, after all!"

"You'll meet her soon enough," sneered another. "I think she'll like you two. You'll make a lovely dessert."

Laughing, the worm lizards moved away.

Max punched the thick skin angrily, but couldn't budge it an inch. Suddenly, a voice from behind made him start.

"Good to see you again, Max. Although I do really wish it had been under better circumstances."

Max spun around. There, hovering in the air, was the source of the light he'd seen shining through the skin.

"Glower! You're alive!"

"For now," Glower said. "They are keeping us imprisoned for a reason—and it's not a very nice one. We're going to be Lieutenant Titan's first meal."

"We?" Max asked.

"Yes," said Glower. "It's not just us who got ourselves captured, I'm afraid."

Out of the shadows, two fearsome-looking insects emerged. They looked like huge blue-black wasps. Their wings were a rusty color, and their long legs ended in hooked claws. Max thought they looked like ninjas. He knew the bugs were his friends, but these two looked downright sinister.

"Let me introduce two members of the underground intelligence service," Glower said. "They are tarantula hawks—flying insects with a powerful sting. Max, meet Nightshade and Dagger."

"Which one's which?" Max asked.

"That is not your concern," the two tarantula hawks said together, in voices just above a whisper.

Roxy shuddered. Max decided not to ask them any more questions.

"Max?" Roxy piped up. "I'm sorry I got us into this mess. I shouldn't have made a noise and alerted those horrible worm lizards."

"It's all right," Max said. "But why were you so scared? Who is this Lieutenant Titan, anyway?"

"She's a myth on Bug Island," Roxy said. "None of us have ever seen her in the flesh, but the stories have been passed down from our ancestors' time. She's one of the Old Ones, like Slimer."

"You mean . . . another prehistoric creature? A living fossil?"

"Yes, a snake. A titanoboa. One of the largest and fiercest reptiles that ever lived."

Max looked at the piece of shed skin that the lizards had used to keep them imprisoned, and felt his throat closing up with dread. Lieutenant Titan must be *huge*.

"Yes, we've all heard the stories, and none of us wants to meet the real thing," said Glower. "If we don't get out of here quickly, we're done for. Any ideas, Max?"

Max couldn't think of anything. He wished Slimer had been there. The old snail might be a little odd, but at least they'd been able to hide in his shell.

"I might have an idea," Roxy said suddenly.

"What is it?" Max asked.

"General Barton didn't just pick me for my bright skin, did he? There's my toxicity, too! I can ooze cyanide from my skin. Poison hurts living creatures, and that doorway's made of snakeskin, which came from a living creature. Maybe my poison will weaken it enough to break?"

Nightshade and Dagger exchanged glances. Glower looked hopeful. "It's all we've got."

"Let's try it," Max said.

Roxy scuttled over to the snakeskin barrier and climbed up onto it, clinging with all her many legs. She squeezed poison out of her body, shivering with the effort. Max stepped back in case any splashed on him.

"That's as much as I can manage," she said.

Max tried to scrape at the bubbling poison patch with his screwdriver. He managed to poke a few holes in the covering, but mostly it was too tough.

"If someone can just help me up, maybe I can—" Max began. Suddenly, he was interrupted.

"I think we're about to have company," Glower hissed. "Listen!"

A distant sound reached them, like someone dragging heavy cloth over a gravelly floor. It grew louder and louder. Roxy trembled. Glower's light flickered fearfully. A vast shadow appeared on the other side of the snakeskin doorway.

"It's her," Roxy said in a quavering voice.

They retreated to the very back of the cave. Then came the sound of the worm lizards moving the rocks out of the way.

The snakeskin was drawn aside and Max

was suddenly looking into a gigantic eye: a terrible, ancient eye with a vertical-slit pupil that was staring right back at him.

Max swallowed. There was only one reptile this could be—*Lieutenant Titan!*

FACING THE ENEMY

Lieutenant Titan slowly pushed her head through the opening. It was almost as large as General Longtooth's had been, and he was a crocodile. Max couldn't imagine the size of the body that must be behind it.

"Iss . . . thiss . . . allll?" she rumbled, in a voice so loud and deep that it shook the cave walls. "You woke me from my sslumber to offer me this meassly assssortment of bugss?"

"Sorry, Mighty One," groveled one of the worm lizards. "This is just an appetizer, to get you started. The real feast is up on the surface!"

"Are they any good? I cannot remember. I have not tassted bugss in many yearss," said Lieutenant Titan dreamily. Her head edged forward even farther. Her forked tongue flickered out menacingly.

Max and the bugs pressed back against the rock wall. There was nowhere left to run.

"Bugs are delicious!" insisted the worm lizard. "Just gobble up these, and you'll soon remember. Then you can lead the reptile army to greatness!"

"They had better be deliciouss, or I shall eat you insstead!" snapped the immense snake. The worm lizards shrank away in fear.

Suddenly, Max realized what was happening. When Titan got a taste for bugs once more, the reptiles would advance on Bug Island under her command. With the snake on the lizards' side, the Battle Bug army would be finished.

Lieutenant Titan swung her head back and forth, looking carefully at the bugs in front of her as if she was wondering where to start. Then she fixed her gaze right on Max. "Ah, strange little bug. You shall have the honor of being my firsst meal in centuriess!"

Her broad, muscular body surged into the cave like an oncoming subway train. Her jaws opened wide. She lunged at him.

Max dived out of the way. Lieutenant Titan's monstrous jaws chomped the air where he had been moments ago. Being tiny had one big advantage; he was nimble and could dodge fast.

Lieutenant Titan shook her head as if she was groggy and trying to wake up. Her cold, unblinking eyes swiveled around, trying to find him. "Sstrange bug? Where did you go?"

Glower yelled, "Nightshade! Dagger! Protect Max!"

The two tarantula hawks took to the air. They flew at Titan's face in a bold attack, jabbing at her eyes with their fearsome, long stingers.

Titan hissed in anger. She snapped at them, but they danced back out of her reach.

Together they began a daring team assault, with one of the pair zooming in close to bombard her with stings, then withdrawing to let the other one attack from a different direction. Titan swung her head back and forth between them, unable to track both at once.

"They can buy us some time," Glower said, "but not long. We need to get out of here."

But there seemed to be no way out. Titan's body almost filled the whole tunnel.

Max suddenly realized that Titan's size could work against her. The prison cave was hardly big enough to hold her head, let alone her whole body.

"She doesn't have enough room to turn around! We *can* get out of here. We just have to run alongside her body faster than she can pull her head back."

"It's worth a try," said Roxy.

"Let's do this!" agreed Glower.

Max ran. He sprinted right underneath Lieutenant Titan's lower jaw. A waft of her breath smelled horrendous, like something moldy found underneath a fridge. He dodged the snapping jaws and ran down into the crevice between her flank and the rock wall. Roxy and Glower followed close behind, with Nightshade and Dagger after them.

Max heard Titan give a furious hiss. "Trickssy bugs! You won't get away from me that eassily!"

The great scaly body began to move, sliding back along the tunnel. Max prayed she didn't roll to the side or they'd all be crushed against the rocky walls.

"She's backing up!" Max cried. "We can still make it. We just need to go faster than she can turn around!"

The worm lizards tried to follow, but Titan's bulk meant they had nowhere to turn.

Titan's body was sliding out of the tunnel faster and faster. Max felt cool air on his face. The cavern with the pools was just up ahead. He could see the rest of Lieutenant Titan coiled up in front of him, a mountain of muscular flesh. She was like a dinosaur, almost too big to be real.

One by one they scrambled out of the tunnel and into the cavern beyond. Max spotted the larger tunnel they'd originally come in through. "This way!" he yelled.

Behind them, Lieutenant Titan withdrew her head all the way. She looked around the cavern. Max thought for a second that she wouldn't spot them, but Glower's shining body gave them away. She came slithering toward them with a triumphant hiss.

"She's still coming," Roxy cried.

They headed up the slope and down the other side. Titan was gaining on them. Max pounded down the tunnel and saw Slimer's shell blocking the way ahead, right where they'd left him.

"Slimer, *move*!" he shouted.

"Is that you, Max? Back already? Just give me a minute."

"We don't have a moment! Lieutenant Titan's right behind us and she's hungry!"

Slimer hastily pulled his shell out of the way.

Gasping, Max stumbled out of the tunnel and into the stalactite cave. His sneakers made stretchy, squelchy noises in Slimer's slime trail. Glower came out, then Roxy, scurrying desperately on all her legs. Behind them all were the two flying tarantula hawks, with Titan's monstrous face filling the whole tunnel behind them.

Nightshade and Dagger flew out of the tunnel like fighter jets. Titan shoved her head out of the opening—and stopped only a little way out.

"She's stuck," Max said in awe.

"I can sstill reach you, bug!" she snarled.

Titan spread her jaws and lunged at Max. He tried to dodge like he had before, but the rocky, uneven floor sent him stumbling. He fought to stand up as Titan bore down on him.

Then, to his amazement, Slimer was there by his side. The ancient snail shoved his long, pointed shell up at Titan like a knight brandishing a lance. Titan hissed and recoiled.

"Get back, you miserable reptile!" bellowed Slimer.

Titan chuckled and then began to laugh out loud. "A *ssnail* challengess me? Me? The very oldesst of nightmaress? You are a fool."

"Save your breath for fighting," Slimer said, and he spun around on the spot in his patch of slime. His shell whacked Titan across the face as hard as a club. Titan swayed back and forth, stunned by the blow.

Slimer swung his shell again. It jabbed her inside the mouth and made her screech with pain. Titan hissed, and moved her body back down the tunnel.

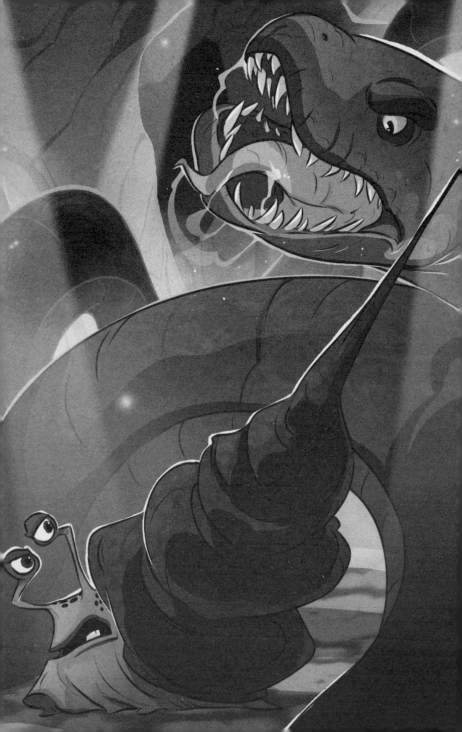

"Thiss issn't the lasst you'll hear from me, bugss!" she hissed as she disappeared back into the darkness.

"Slimer, that was incredible!" Max yelled.

"There's still some life in this old snail, yet," Slimer huffed proudly. "You little ones get to the surface! I'll guard this exit to the tunnel. If she dares to come back, she'll have me to deal with."

Max hesitated. "But which way do we go?"

"Don't you remember? Turn right, then straight ahead, then the third tunnel on the left, and when you reach the big root, go straight ahead!"

Max could only hope instinct would send him in the right direction.

"Thanks, Slimer," said Max. "We couldn't have done this without you."

"No problem, little Max," he said. "Now get out of here before that big brute comes back."

Max didn't need telling twice. With Glower and Roxy lighting the way, they delved into the labyrinth of tunnels once more.

ESCAPE ROUTE

"Straight ahead at the big root," Max repeated to himself as he and the bugs ran down the tunnel.

"Max! Is that light up ahead?" Roxy asked.

Max paused and peered into the distance. Sure enough, a dim light was filtering through into the underground world.

"Come on!" he yelled, running forward with fresh energy.

Slimer had pointed them in the right direction after all. They ran out into the cavern they had descended into earlier. Welcome daylight poured down from above.

"Look at that!" Max laughed. "We were down there for so long, it's daytime now!"

The ground vibrated under his feet.

"Uh-oh," Roxy said. "Titan must have found another way out. I think she still wants her meal."

"Dagger! Nightshade!" Glower barked. "Fly up and prepare a welcoming party. If Lieutenant Titan makes it to the surface, we need to give her a proper Battle Bugs welcome."

"Yes, sir!" the tarantula hawks buzzed as they quickly flew up to the surface.

Max strained to see if Webster was still up there, but there was no sign of the spider. He hoped he'd see his friend safe and sound again. Then a terrible thought struck him.

"Roxy, you can climb up the side of the wall, and Glower can fly, but without Webster's webbing line, how am I going to get out?"

"That's easy," Glower said. "I'll carry you."

The ground shuddered again, more strongly this time. A distant hiss echoed through the tunnels.

"How?" Max asked. As the ground rumbled, he felt the same creeping sense of anticipation he used to feel on the subway platform when he was little, palms tingling, waiting for the train to come rushing out of the dark. Back then he'd been excited. Now he was afraid.

"You can hang on to my legs," said Glower. "It'll be easy."

Max figured there was no other choice, so he grabbed hold of two of Glower's spindly legs, while Roxy took two on the other side. The firefly glanced anxiously at a wide tunnel mouth just across the cave and lifted off into the air. He groaned with the effort of carrying so much cargo.

Suddenly, Lieutenant Titan's monstrous head loomed from the tunnel behind them.

Her pupils shrank as the daylight hit them. She hissed in annoyance.

"THERE you are!"

Glower struggled to lift Max and Roxy, but he was barely off the ground.

Titan snapped at him. The light dazzled her, and that was all that saved Max and the bugs. She missed, narrowly. Glower flew back with a cry, struck the wall, and dropped his passengers.

Max acted fast, scrambling to his feet and dodging behind the nearest rocky outcrop.

He and Roxy cowered there while Titan nosed around the cavern, searching for them. Glower immediately took to the air

once more, dancing around Titan's head in an attempt to distract her. However, Titan seemed more interested in Max.

"Come to me," she murmured. "I want to devour you, sstrange bug. Are you deliciouss? I hope so . . ."

"We're doomed," Roxy gasped, hiding her face. But Max felt a sudden surge of hope. An idea was forming in his mind.

"Roxy, can you do your thing with the cyanide?" he asked.

"I can try," Roxy said. "But if I get close to her, she'll snap me up!"

"Maybe we don't need to get close to her," Max said craftily.

"I don't get it!"

Max took his hoodie back from Roxy and quickly grabbed a few rocks that were lying around. "Cover this with your poison," he said, passing her one. "As much as you can manage."

Overhead, Glower was flying around and around Titan's head like a frantic satellite. She snapped angrily at him, but he darted away each time.

Roxy busily covered the rock with poison. "There," she said.

"Awesome!" Max said, as he wrapped the poisoned rock carefully in his hoodie. The hoodie would keep Roxy's poison from touching his skin—and hopefully play another important role, too.

He took a deep breath and stepped out of hiding.

"Looking for me, you slithering monster?" he yelled.

Titan swung her head around to face him. "You dare inssult me?"

"You want to find out how I taste?" Max jeered. "Come and find out!" He flung one of his rocks. It bounced off Titan's nose. She winced.

"Max, what are you DOING?" Roxy cried. "She'll eat you!"

"She can try," Max said, throwing another rock. This one smacked Titan in the eye.

"DIE, SSTRANGE BUG!" roared Titan. She spread her jaws wide and lunged.

Max threw his hoodie, rock and all, right into her jaws. He dived aside as Titan snatched it out of the air, gulped, and swallowed.

Max hid behind the rock again, not daring to breathe, as Titan's long tongue came out and licked her lips.

"Got you," she hissed in satisfaction.

Then she paused, and a strange look came over her face . . .

A TITAN DEFEAT

While Lieutenant Titan stood motionless, Glower took his chance. He came in on a swooping dive.

Max and Roxy caught hold of the firefly's legs. Straining with all his might, he carried them up into the air. They rose up and up, until they were right over Titan's head.

Titan slowly looked up at them. "What have you done?" she hissed. "This is disgusting! Is this what bug tastes like? How could I ever have thought this was delicious?"

"She may be big," Roxy whispered to Max, "but she's not very bright, is she?"

Titan swayed. Her eyes seemed to bulge out of her head and her face showed confusion, then sudden rage. She reared up, her whole body writhing in anger. Her enormous mouth yawned open, ready to snap shut.

"Glower, get us out of here, now!" Max yelled.

Glower flew like fury. Roxy's long body dangled above Titan's gaping mouth.

Max could see all the way down inside her yawning throat, like a tunnel made of flesh. He wondered how many creatures had vanished forever down that horrible gullet. Something her size could probably swallow a crocodile with room to spare. No wonder the other reptiles, like the worm lizards, were scared of her, too.

Titan's body just kept on uncoiling and reaching farther up. She was gaining on them.

Glower gasped. His wings faltered. A look of triumph came into Titan's eyes.

"Keep going, Glower," Max cried.

The next moment, without warning, Titan's terrifying eyes seemed to glaze over. Her whole body stiffened.

"The poison!" Roxy yelled. "I think it's working!"

"I feel . . . ssick," she said. "What . . . have you . . . done to me?"

"We've beaten you," said Max.

"Imposssssible! Nothing as tiny as you could ever . . . could . . . ever . . ."

Titan wobbled back and forth like a great tree that was about to come crashing down.

Glower made one final effort. He flew the last few feet and collapsed on the edge of the hole, his legs and wings in a jumble. Max and Roxy went tumbling across the ground. Max sprang to his feet and was pleased to see Dagger, Nightshade, and a small army of warrior bugs heading their way.

Titan's head rose slowly out of the pit.

She strained to reach Max. But before she could open her mouth, her eyes rolled back into her head. Her entire body went limp and loose. Her head fell and whacked on the edge of the hole.

Roxy tried to hold him back, but Max leaned over the edge to see. Titan was collapsing like a demolished building, her long body falling in limp coils. She lay in a motionless heap. Max held his breath to see what would happen next.

Slowly, painfully, Titan began the crawl back into the dark tunnels. "Ssleep," she murmured to herself. "Ssssleep . . ."

"I don't think Lieutenant Titan's feeling very well," Max said. "Poor thing. She needs a long rest."

"Another few thousand years ought to do the trick!" Roxy laughed.

Max and Roxy walked back to the bug camp, surrounded by excited, happy bugs. Nightshade and Dagger carried Glower, who was too exhausted to move.

"Good work down there, Cadet Roxy," Glower whispered, his light down to a feeble glimmer. "Have you ever considered a career in underground intelligence?"

Roxy lit up with pride. "Dreamed of it all my life, sir."

"Well. I'd better speak to Barton, hadn't I? It's about time you were promoted."

They arrived to a thunderous welcome at the bug camp. Hundreds of bugs had turned out to greet the heroes of the day, with

General Barton leading the applause. Spike came scuttling up, followed by Webster, to Max's relief.

"You made it!" Max yelled, giving the spider a happy hug.

"Spike saved my life," Webster admitted. "He heard me shouting, left his patrol, and came running over. Between us, we chased those worm lizards halfway across Bug Island!"

"Spike, we'll have to add the Misty Marshes to our patrol route in the future," Barton said gruffly. "Now we know what's under that part of Bug Island, we'll need to keep a careful watch on it. There are creatures deep underground that we must consider fearsome enemies."

"There are some fearsome friends down there, too," Max said, thinking of Slimer. If it weren't for him, they'd never have made it out of there.

Suddenly, though, he felt a familiar tugging feeling on his arms and legs that meant it was time to go home.

"Bye, Battle Bugs," he called hastily. "Until next time!"

Suddenly, he felt his whole body being pulled up into the sky, as the bugs wished him farewell. Before he knew it, he was being thrown out of the encyclopedia. He landed back in his room, just in time to hear his dad calling for him up the stairs.

"Coming!" he shouted, as he grabbed the makeshift snail eyestalks that would be attached to his soapbox. He glanced at his one empty bug tank.

"Some tropical snails are just what I need to liven that tank up," he said aloud to himself.

"Come on, snail boy, hurry up!" he heard his dad shout.

Max raced downstairs and out into his dad's SUV. A short while later, he was lined up on the starting block for the soapbox race. Max held on tight to the steering rope, ready to go.

The slope was even steeper than he'd expected, but he thought of his strange adventures under the tunnels of Bug Island, and soon courage ran through his veins.

"If I can fight off a giant snake, I can win this race," he whispered.

Then, a shot rang out from the marshal's starting pistol, and Max launched himself down the hill.

REAL LIFE BATTLE BUGS!

Sierra luminous millipedes (*Motyxia*)

The sierra luminous millipede, or *Motyxia*, is a genus of millipede with an unusual and distinctive ability. These millipedes are bioluminescent, which means they can glow in the dark!

Normally, insects try to stay away from predators, so it seems odd that the sierra luminous millipede would advertise itself by lighting up. However, scientists believe its special ability is a strong warning to stay away. These millipedes have a power-ful trick up their sleeves: poison, and a lot of it.

They are able to secrete toxic cyanide from their skin. Just one bite of one of these millipedes would kill a would-be predator. The millipedes' glow acts as a stop sign of sorts. It tells predators that these insects are not good to eat—and that they might just be deadly!

Giant snail (*Campanile giganteum*)

One of the largest species of snail that has ever existed is the *Campanile giganteum*, or the giant snail. This snail lived way back in Earth's past in a geological era known as the Eocene. It's shell could be anywhere between fifteen and twenty-three inches long.

Back then, 56 to 33.9 million years ago, life as we know it was completely different. Early on in the Eocene period the earth would have been much warmer than it is today and forests would have covered much of its land mass. Early mammals, such as primates, rodents, and marsupials, were much smaller than their present day coun- terparts. As for the sea-dwelling giant snail, the warm temperatures and different mixtures of gases in the atmosphere (much more methane and carbon dioxide than in today's world), meant it could grow to an impressive size.

One present-day snail species is even larger than the extinct giant snail: the *Syrinx aruanus*, or Australian trumpet. This species lives in the waters off northern Australia and Indonesia. Australian trumpet shells as long as thirty-five inches have been found!

JOIN THE RACE!

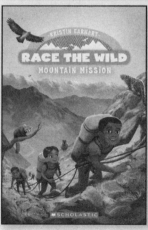

It's an incredible adventure through the animal kingdom, as kids zip-line, kayak, and scuba dive their way to the finish line! Packed with cool facts about amazing creatures, dangerous habitats, and more!

MEET RANGER

A time–traveling golden retriever with search-and-rescue training . . . and a nose for danger!

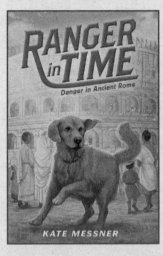